BABY RHINO MORENO, THE FIGHT FOR JUSTICE (1)

A FANTASY I DREAM WILL COME TRUE ONE DAY

Baby Rhino Moreno

AuthorHouse™ UK
1663 Liberty Drive
Bloomington, IN 47403 USA
www.authorhouse.co.uk
UK TFN: 0800 0148641 (Toll Free inside the UK)
UK Local: 02036 956322 (+44 20 3695 6322 from outside the UK)

Cover by Mrs. Trupti Shah
Author: Mr. Rajesh Shah
Edited by: Mr Rajesh Shah and Trupti Shah

ISBN: 978-1-6655-8411-1 (sc)
ISBN: 978-1-6655-8410-4 (e)

Print information available on the last page.

Published by AuthorHouse 04/09/2021

authorHOUSE®

This is dedicated to Trupti Shah, my beloved wife. Before I talk about the story, I would like to share with you my aims for writing this book. Firstly, I have always had a lifelong love to help and protect rhinos and elephants from the cruel, barbaric and greedy human pests who constantly poach them. Secondly, I want to do something to help alleviate the pain and suffering of so many people who have been affected by the Covid-19 virus. All of the proceeds earned from the sale of this book will go to these two causes.

The best experience, a dream come true, was firstly, the sight of the rhino, truly an exciting adventure for me, at Ol Pejeta. Secondly, then approaching, the love of my life, on foot, the rhino bowed down, and sat down, to allow me to climb on to the back, being the biggest thrill, I had ever experienced in my life!

Contents

Acknowledgements

This is my first attempt to compose a narration that I believe is a celebration of a subject that has been my inspiration, deeply rooted inside my grey matter, since 1964 when I was only a wee 4-year-old.

I would like to express my appreciation for the unconditional support given by my wife, who inspired me to write this story and helped me prepare the cover and achieve its publication.

I am also grateful to my papa,Prabhulal Jivraj Kara Shah who was an enthusiastic movie buff and, curiously enough, conveniently fitted me into all his regular weekend plans as a devoted fan.

Preface

In 1964, I saw a blockbuster Hollywood wildlife film called *Hatari* (a Swahili term meaning 'danger'[1]), filmed in a game park near a rural town called Arusha in Tanzania. John Wayne, my boyhood hero, a Geronimo of the Wild West, played the starring role.

John Wayne was famous particularly as a cowboy, and because of that, I always wanted to wear corduroy to imitate my boyhood hero. Being a versatile actor, he starred in this movie with a virtuoso performance, par excellence and of importance as always. He is sadly no longer with us, but the memories still linger on forevermore. I understand this was the first and only wildlife film that John Wayne ever starred in. There are breathtaking shots of various animals being trapped, such as zebras, giraffes, buffalos, gazelles, and so on, after exhilarating chases. More importantly, there is one particularly exciting rhinoceros capture, the movie's most thrilling scene, a contest of trapping one but not without a thrilling fight. Howard Hawks, the director of this film, was inspired to use a specially designed automobile, which made me squeal. There is one remarkable scene with a so-called 'Indian' who is wounded by the rhinoceros, whose horn pierces his thigh whilst he is sitting in the front seat of the open four-wheel drive. He was fortunate to be alive and survive.

At first, I used to hate the rhinoceros for injuring the man, but, gradually, as my understanding grew more, I realised that this was actually meant to be really very heart-warming for me, as the poor rhino gets his or her revenge for the constant barrage of atrocities the poor soul has to suffer. To me, the rhino chase is like a poacher trapping his kill, just to get a cheap thrill, no doubt, to also fulfil a heinous act of cruelty and inhumanity.

The film also has a melodious musical direction by Henry Mancini, especially with the haunting and simultaneously enviously flaunting melody of the night shots of the vehicle returning back home after a day's successful animal hunt.

'Baby Elephant Walk' is a song written in 1961 by Henry Mancini for the 1962 film. In 1963, the song earned Mancini a well-deserved Grammy Award for Best Instrumental Arrangement, no doubt because it is an exhilarating tune which is also reinvigorating, written for a spur-of-the-moment scene in the film. This creates a stir in which 'Dallas' (Elsa Martinelli) led three baby elephants to a waterhole to lunge for a hilarious plunge.

An illustration of a scene showing the animal
trappers in the specially designed vehicle.

Chapter 1

Papa Kifu and Papa Rajah

In the deep forests of Kenya along the Aberdare Range is a 160-kilometre-(100-mile) long mountain range, north of Kenya's capital city, Nairobi. It has an average elevation of 3,500 metres (11,480 feet). The Agikuyu people, in whose territory this forest and mountain range are located, call the mountain range Nyandarua.[2] Here, there once lived two lifelong buddies, a cute rhinoceros named Kifu and a shy, warm, loving elephant called Rajah.

Kifu had a boisterous wife, Sita, and a fun-loving little baby called Moreno.

Rajah had an equally delightful family with a very devoted wife called Rani and an overactive baby, Ganesh.

Moreno and Ganesh became bosom pals.

One early morning, when Kifu's and Rajah's families were fast asleep, they both secretly crept out of their abode in search of fresh water to drink, quickly becoming a scarcity because of an ongoing drought. The deluge of rain that usually came around this time of the year seemed to have abandoned them, causing a severe strain.

Rajah and Kifu ambled side by side like brothers, trampling the rocky, uneven terrain. When Kifu and Rajah were about three miles from home, they stumbled onto a clearing fringed by a rich, abundant growth of young, sweet, pungent, and juicy trees. There was also a welcoming gurgling sound of water barely audible to them but no doubt a plausible thought. The noise seemed to be coming from under their feet.

Whilst they were busy looking for the source of this gurgling sound, suddenly, there was a terrific crashing noise, disturbing them and leaving both Rajah and Kifu stunned and frozen in their poses.

Three masked men in black balaclavas, holding what seemed like machetes, a machine gun, and a huge chain saw with a powerful jaw surrounded Kifu and Rajah, chanting and ranting 'Red Indian'-type wails, feeling merry and looking very scary. With very swift blows of the machetes, sadly, Kifu and Rajah both found themselves gasping for their last breaths whilst facing imminent death. Poor Kifu crashed to the ground with his beautiful horns slashed, leaving rich red blood gushing forth to form a stream. It is hard to imagine. Rajah was left without a trunk, which was detached by the whirring chain saw, the beautiful ivory tusks ripped out as he slowly sank to the ground. Kifu and Rajah were no more.

Circling above was a flock of black vultures. They were making raspy, drawn-out hissing sounds along with grunting noises that sounded like hungry pigs or dogs barking in the distance, getting ready to devour their feast.

Rajah and Kifu Slaughtered

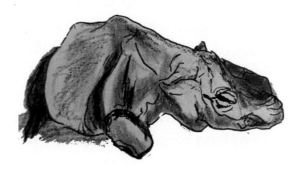

Kifu with his horns violently slashed off

Rajah, the majestic beast, with his head cut in half
to remove his tusks with the chainsaw

Chapter 2

Rani and Sita

Rani and Sita were up at the crack of dawn but not without a sneaky yawn, as the white, yellow, and orange stream of light filtered onto their current home, a 20-year-old acacia tree with foliage that was typically bright green or bluish-green. More important, the tree was sheltered away from the intense heat in the summer, being a perfect retreat situated against a tall hillside.

Both babies were in a deep slumber in the midsummer heat. Sita was very restless and wondered where Kifu and Rajah were. Sita convinced Rani that they should go and see if they could locate their dear hubbies. They silently sneaked away from the acacia tree.

'Let's hope we can find them quickly before the heat gets sticky and our beloved boys wake up,' said Rani.

An idea came into Rani's mind. She knew how to find their hubbies' whereabouts. 'Let's look for fresh elephant and rhino droppings. That will indicate which way they have gone.'

Sita gave Rani a big smile and retorted that it was a brilliant idea which had never occurred to her.

So off they went before they could change their minds with the intent of finding their husbands. Yes, how right Rani was! Slowly but surely, as they were trotting along, they did come across some fresh droppings of elephant and rhino faeces being merrily swarmed by a gathering of bluebottle flies. This was about a kilometre and a half (one mile) away from home. They headed for the rocky outcrop area near the cloud top.

Then, yes, as they neared the rocky outcrop, the dense forest thinned, and Rani and Sita sensed the same gushing sound of water their hubbies had.

They then stumbled onto the boys about three miles away. They looked with horror at the area stained red, as they witnessed the horrendous massacre of the barbaric, meaningless slaughter.

Rani gathering the tree limbs with juicy leaves

Rani trumpeted loudly and angrily but remorsefully, whilst Sita bellowed with tears running down her cheeks. She dared not look at the remains of their dear husbands. At first, seeing the severed head of her beloved hubby, Rani could not believe that it was her beloved Rajah. Then she got closer. She could barely look at the thick reddish-brown blood streaking where the beautiful tusks used to be. The half-open ghostly eyes stared at her, and she began to feel sick. Sita couldn't bear to look at Kifu's lifeless carcass.

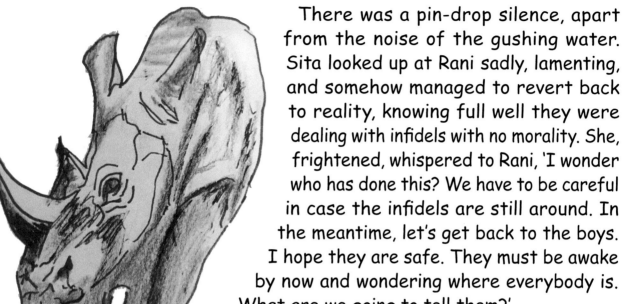

Sita

There was a pin-drop silence, apart from the noise of the gushing water. Sita looked up at Rani sadly, lamenting, and somehow managed to revert back to reality, knowing full well they were dealing with infidels with no morality. She, frightened, whispered to Rani, 'I wonder who has done this? We have to be careful in case the infidels are still around. In the meantime, let's get back to the boys. I hope they are safe. They must be awake by now and wondering where everybody is. What are we going to tell them?'

Rani was very morose as well, but she still had the strength to put her trunk round Sita to comfort her. 'I think the best thing is to just go back and act as if everything is normal. We don't want to see them upset. I will clutch a few juicy tree limbs in my trunk for the boys. They must be ravenous and starving.'

'You know what Moreno is like when he wakes up in the morning,' Sita woefully murmured. A sad Rani and Sita dragged themselves to the boys.

Chapter 3

Breakfast

The boys were getting up when Rani and Sita arrived. Their moms knew full well they were lucky to have survived.

Moreno was still feeling a bit groggy but no doubt as cocky as always from having a late night staying awake chatting with his two mates, Robbie and Ganesh.

'Mum, what's for breakfast?' asked Moreno.

Sita stepped up near her darling son and prompted Rani to drop the juicy limbs by his feet, ready to eat.

'Look how good my mum is, buddy!' Ganesh smiled at Moreno. 'Thank you, Mum. I could eat a horse!' he trumpeted.

Both of them dug in and gobbled down most of the juicy leaves despite all the fleas continuously irritating them.

Then, suddenly, Moreno looked up at his mum and asked her, 'Where is Dad?'

Sita was taken aback but just remembered to remain calm and get a hold of herself. Looking toward Rani, she uttered, 'Dad and Rajah are busy looking for some water for us, darling. Hopefully, they will be back soon, with some good news. You well know we are facing a severe drought at the moment.'

Rani and Sita had thus far managed to keep their children occupied within themselves, but deep inside, there was a growing fear. For how much longer could they hide the truth?

***

The boys were busy chatting with each other, planning the day's activity. They, as always, had already planned their day. Ganesh trumpeted the familiar tune in hopes of getting Robbie to join them.

'Today, being scorching hot, I thought a dip in the local pool would be a smart plot!' Moreno grinned. He would love a wallow and also a roll to cool down in a mud bath.

Moreno and Ganesh were lucky to have this luxury not far away.

They were soon greeted by a sweet tweet from Robbie.

Baby rhinos sound adorable, like a cross between a whale's call and when you pinch the neck of a balloon to let the air out. The sound of a baby elephant 'giggling' is the sound of pure, unfiltered joy.

The three buddies were in good spirits, pleased with their wits.

Chapter 4

The Confession of Kifu's and Rajah's Predicament

After breakfast, Moreno and Ganesh were summoned by their dear mums to come and sit by them. Feeling guilty, both mamas could not hold the sad news from their beloved boys any longer.

'We have something to tell you both. We don't know how to put this to you, but finally, we have built up the courage to face you both. We are sorry we lied. Believe me, we had no intention to decide that, but honestly, we also know you will have great animosity. We just didn't know how to tell you, being in shock ourselves,' Rani began.

Sita continued, 'Unfortunately, your papas sneaked out last night without our knowledge whilst we were slumbering to search for water for all of us. Whilst they were searching for the water, it seems they were attacked by the dreaded poachers, or so called "pests" you know we all detest.

'This happened a few miles from here. We discovered their mangled bodies, and the sight was obnoxious. We did not want to upset you but now feel that you should know. We are very sorry to tell you this. There is a horrible world out there, and we want to protect you from these infidels.'

On hearing this, Moreno's facial expression changed as if he were being strangled. He started fuming, and his eyes boiled red. The next minute, he was a totally different being, like a monster! He fled, running away from the acacia tree.

Moreno fuming

He was acrimonious and enraged, not at all his usual harmonious self.

Just then, the baby robin Robbie flew toward him, looking very grim. Robbie lived on the acacia tree and had developed a close relationship with Moreno and Ganesh. After seeing Moreno in this state, he approached him to try to calm him. He noticed there was something drastically wrong.

Why is Moreno so upset? Is he threatened? Robbie wondered.

'What's the matter?' asked Robbie.

At first, on seeing Robbie, Moreno did not say anything about his burst of temper, but eventually, he slowly but surely calmed himself down after realising it was no other but his great friend Robbie, who just wanted to see him feel better.

He then, feeling a bit ashamed, explained everything quickly to Robbie, coughing and spluttering at the same time he was talking about the most heinous crime and how barbarically both the dads, Kifu and Rajah, had been attacked by poachers. He was traumatised.

Robbie, being what he was, first of all, put his warm feathered wings round Moreno, giving him instant relief against the atrocious stings of life. He instilled such confidence and reassured both of them that those dreadful murderers would be brought to justice to pay for all their dastardly deeds.

Robbie vowed, 'You can be reassured indeed, because I will proceed immediately to my lifelong mate to inform him of your predicament. He lives high up in the mountain and will no doubt come up with a solution, which will be your retribution.'

Baby Rhino Moreno

Baby Elephant Ganesh

Baby Robin Robbie

Chapter 5

Baby Rhino Moreno, Baby Elephant Ganesh, and Baby Robin Robbie: The Three Amigos

I am now going to digress and brief you about the three mates pictured above.

They are more popularly known as 'the three amigos'. They are always cuddled and huddled up near the acacia tree. Moreno is always grumbling, and Ganesh is always stumbling to a sympathetic, mumbling Robbie. That is a typical scenario of the three.

Moreno spent a lot of time with his mates and grew up to be a fine, confident, fun-loving 4-year-old. There was no doubt he had an extra-special sensory quality but also great gusto and frivolity.

Baby Ganesh was a strange acquaintance, holding Moreno's lasting obedience.

One day, Ganesh and his mama and papa, along with a group of his cousins, uncles, and aunts stopped near the acacia tree. Ganesh, with glee, immediately set out to make instant friends with Moreno and Robbie, one has to agree.

Baby Robbie was a resident of the acacia tree. He was one of six brothers and sisters. He would fly out to meet Moreno and Ganesh every day. They happened to be just a few minutes away, down the tree.

This was the permanent residence of Moreno and his family, Ganesh and his family, and, last but not least, Robbie himself. There was a precedent to living in a secure environment, but little did anyone know that both Moreno and Ganesh would suffer a horrible catastrophe.

***

Coming back to today, a true bond of friendship had formed between Moreno, Ganesh, and Robbie. They were no doubt inseparable, their friendship being naturally inevitable.

Both Moreno and Ganesh silently listened to Robbie's reassurance of his wonderful friend's support and were convinced and ready to plan an attack in retaliation for the horrific murders of Kifu and Rajah. Wouldn't they love to smother them?

Robbie confidently said that there was no doubt that whatever action his dear mate decided to take, there would definitely be a successful, lasting impact. 'And that's a fact.'

Robbie explained that he would have to leave them for a few days to allow him to contact his friend, who lived near the Mount Kenya slope, confident in his hope of success, I guess.

His friend was none other than a golden eagle called Eddie. He was ready and always steady.

Chapter 6

Baby Robin Robbie Meets His Friend Eddie, the Steady Golden Eagle

Eddie was glad to see Robbie, clad in his bright apparel.

'Hi, buddy! What brings you here?'

Robbie eased himself nearer to his pal and said, 'To be frank, I am here to ask your favour, you being my highly esteemed redeemer to demean the sinners against my dear mates Moreno's and Ganesh's papas.'

He then described the horrible trauma his mates had been through, hoping Eddie would be the one to make a successful breakthrough for his friends, whom he had promised he knew just the aides to perform successful raids.

Eddie

Chapter 7

Eddie Reveals His Barmy Army
of Faithful Soldiers

'Don't you worry, my dear friend,' said Eddie. 'I have a long-serving team of loyal mates of mine who will no doubt assist in teaching these culprits a lesson, with no question.'

Friends of Eddie

Crafty the Owl

Henry the Hawk

Sammie the Falcon

Beaky the Buzzard

Buzzie the Vulture

Crafty the Owl

'This is my most reliable night surveillance expert, being an extrovert, whom I discovered one night by accident. He is also luckily a local inhabitant. This happened when I was swooping around, looking for grub in a shrub for my little babies to nibble with no quibble. I stumbled upon some rats in a grotto hidden in a hollow, and guess what! Sitting quietly in a corner was Crafty merrily gulping a big fat rat! I went towards him, and to my surprise, I find it difficult to surmise, he happily allowed me to join in the feast of the little beast. With my beak, I trapped a few morsels to feed my darling babies. This was the beginning of a true friendship with him. The beauty of Crafty was that he could pinpoint with unarguable accuracy the location of any living being. What I feel is he could be a great asset to us, a plus with no fuss.'

Henry the Hawk

'Henry is also my ever-consistent mate, whom I rate highly. He is a very intelligent instigator of a particular action, always getting a positive reaction. It's interesting to tell you how I came across him.

'One day, whilst flying through the woods, I approached a small gathering of birds near a carcass of a fish. Henry had grabbed half the fish in his beak and was ready to pounce onto the rest of it. I swooped next to him, and he twisted his head round as if he were going to attack me. But, surprisingly, he started twittering to me to welcome me. I was astonished to see someone so polished. But I soon realised just like when I met Crafty that there are plenty of good friends around, so profound.'

Sammie the Falcon

'Sammie is another super-efficient buddy keen to be the understudy of Henry. Thanks to Henry for allowing me to fly with him to meet Sammie in his nest. Henry and Sammie are like Abbott and Costello, Laurel and Hardy, and such, the great comedy duos, coordinating everything they do together with hilarious frivolity.'

Beaky the Buzzard

'Beaky the buzzard is a self-trained master of completing all my actions diligently. It is interesting how we got acquainted. Beaky was flying close to my eyrie. He noticed me, flew inside, and stood beside me. I just happened to be feeding my filial ones. I was aware of the presence of Sammie. At first, I was very reluctant and petrified, but there was nothing to be terrified of. He was just an inquisitive busybody. Sammie decided to observe my feeding technique. I thought this was very mysterious. I soon realised that he was just trying to be friendly, not deadly, but rather kindly and gently, I managed to prompt him to join me, an invitation to which he willingly responded.

'The next thing was he also grabbed pieces of the tasty grub I did not snub. I was pleasantly shocked and from that day on, he has been my understudy every day and a loyal member of my team.'

Buzzie the Vulture

'Last but not least, there is Buzzie, my oldest and most honest friend, I cannot pretend, on whom I always depend. He has served me the longest, being no doubt the strongest in willpower never, ever to protest. I was honoured to meet Buzzie, who always seemed to be in a frenzy. He has served his particular clan, like Peter Pan, and is my fan. With plenty of self-pride, he always takes things in his stride. Everywhere I go, the name Buzzie reverberates and no doubt makes me very elated. I was quick to realise that such an entity would be a great asset, you bet, for my team. I invited Buzzie to my home and, after a hearty meal, offered him a position that's become his ambition to achieve to perceive a status of pride well within his stride. He acts as an organiser of the whole team with members, ensuring everyone remembers their delegated tasks painstakingly legislated.'

Chapter 8

Eddie Finalises the Attack on the Poachers and Informs Robbie

Eddie said, 'I requested my night surveillance expert, Crafty, my faithful vigilante, to identify the secret hideout of the infidels as soon as possible to allow me to commence the attack. Within a short space of time, he came up with some plausible information after scanning the whole region around the Aberdares, being a danger to anyone who dares. He explained to me that they were living with a local tribe. Also, they were definitely the three attackers. Every morning after the sun had set, the three infidels carried out a regular exercise schedule of performing a machete and shooting practice display. If they have to be tackled, we have to be smart. It would have to be with total surprise. This would be a very early-morning attack with guile and tactical expertise to hit them and entirely condemn them.'

Eddie finalised the attack:

The attack on the poachers was going to be done just before dawn broke and well before the poachers were awake. Eddie made the plan with the help of Crafty's helpful research.

'Basically, I will be supervising all the attacks along with Buzzie, my lucky chummy. Firstly, I will instruct Sammie and Henry to be ready to attack directly by swooping down onto each and every poacher and scraping their nasal area cavity quickly and efficiently with their sharp talons and beaks.

'Once, that is complete, Buzzie and Beaky will commence the next stage of action, which is to help clean up the mess of the nasal infiltration and collect all the nasal debris to use as our next meal. The gist of doing this is to teach the infidels a lesson to never have any ideas of hurting any of my animal friends, especially not to ever mess up their pretty faces. I will go to any length to make sure all my fellow friends are given full respect and dignity to stand tall and live with pride whenever and wherever they decide. Now, if you can kindly allow me to go to have my beauty sleep, a discipline I always keep.'

Robbie was very understanding and impressed by the planning. He wished Eddie a good night and the best of luck and told him to sleep tight.

He fluttered his delicate wings and began to sing his favourite tune whilst soaring up into the air, heading toward home, all alone, as the sun shone.

Chapter 9

Robbie Flies Back to His Friends to Inform Them of Eddie's Master Plan

Moreno and Ganesh were glad to see Robbie back. Three whole days had elapsed from when Robbie had left them.

'I have good news for you from Eddie, who was ready to carry out the onslaught, as I was sure he would do anything I requested,' twittered Robbie. Then, Robbie told them of the details of Eddie's so-called 'foolproof plan'.

This left Moreno and Ganesh feeling ecstatic and at the same time emphatic. Robbie had been a real hero, a true pro.

Now, all they had to do was wait for tomorrow and look forward to Eddie's master plan, 'Of which I will become the first fan!' bellowed Moreno.

Chapter 10

The Day of the Annihilation of the Poachers

The resident cockerel, the natural early morning alarm, sang out the familiar tune.

It was the day of annihilation, a hopeful sensation of motivation. Eddie was up very early, looking fresh and ready to impress, ready to marshal his authority on his ever-faithful team of soldiers as they prepared to go to battle and be ready to grapple. One by one, the team members started arriving at Eddie's eyrie. Eddie had collected enough grub, such as juicy worms in a squirm, beetles darting backwards and forwards, grasshoppers—the mini helicopters—and an assorted range of fresh fish to relish. He was a good host, ensuring all his dedicated friends were well fed and looked after and fully energised to master the enterprise.

At about 5 a.m., there was a well-organised stream of 'soldiers' ready to attack the poachers (except Crafty). They were ready to fly in a well-organised attacking unit to the location of the poachers, graphically described by Crafty.

Once they reached the destination after fifteen to twenty minutes of flying, Eddie gathered everyone and told them to get into their intended positions before attacking. He ensured that there was dead silence during an attack on the poachers with the element of total surprise applied.

Sammie and Henry were the first to begin the mission, and after an hour had elapsed, there was a flutter in the camp as the victorious fighters returned proudly, and you could hear everyone uttering the news of a powerful attack resulting in the calamity of the poachers. Eddie had to stress this good news, announcing loudly the message.

Sammie, as expected, loved to be the centre of attention and began reciting to Eddie the intricate details of how the 'Butch Cassidy and Sundance Kid'–type operation was bravely and safely performed.

Now it was time for the second part of the attack, whereby Buzzie and Beaky began their allocated task, and within half an hour, their action was complete. They were hailed with 'peewee-uu' notes, rasping 'cack cack, cack' screaming, 'kee-eeeee-arr,' and raspy, drawn-out hissing sounds just like when heroes arrived. Buzzie and Beaky had brought beakfuls of the scraped-off nasal debris and dropped that down near Eddie's feet to a loud cheer from all the delighted friends.

Eddie was quick to announce another triumphant strike, boasting about it in a businesslike manner. He was keen to inform the amigos of the good news to allay their woes. He knew they must be wondering and maybe pondering about them.

***

Moreno was fast asleep and in the trance of an eerie nightmare, dreaming of a poacher without a nose. The nightmare seemed to make him twist his head to look up to heaven, and that was when he visualised his papa, Kifu, grinning with a broad smile and raising his left paw in a salute to imply to him, 'Well done, my baby.'

To that, Moreno opened his eyes, becoming wide awake, initially in shock, but he soon realised that he was only dreaming.

It was not until the next day when the towering, empowering, familiar figure of Eddie smiling stood next to him. He said that he had sensational and inspirational news of three most wanted poachers with blood-stricken faces. It seemed like their noses had been violently ripped off by unknown entities. To that, Moreno jumped up with a nice feeling inside, thinking that what he had dreamt was actually a reality and knowing full well that it was Eddie who was the real hero in his eyes. At least his papa's death was avenged at last!

He saw Ganesh doing a jig and Robbie whistling a happy tune.

Rani and Sita were amazed by the story in this hot news, not having an inkling but at the same time seeing a twinkling in their sons' eyes.

A Drawing Showing a Poacher Stripped of His Nose

Watch out for the next thrilling adventure of the three amigos!

Endnotes

(Endnotes)

[1] *Hatari*, Howard Hawks, dir., Paramount Pictures, 1962.
[2] Wikipedia, s.v. 'Aberdare Range', https://en.wikipedia.org/wiki/Aberdare_Range; Wikipedia, s.v. 'Great Rift Valley,' https://en.wikipedia.org/wiki/Great_Rift_Valley.